For Marlis and Brigitte

Copyright © 1983 Nord-Süd Verlag, Mönchaltorf and Hamburg
English text © 1983 Abelard-Schuman Ltd
First published in the United States of America 1983 by
Faber & Faber Inc.,
39 Thompson Street, Winchester, MA 01890

Library of Congress Cataloging in Publication Data
Damjan, Mischa, pseud.
    The Little Sea Horse.
    Translation of Pony das Seepferdchen.
Summary: Pony and his friends undertake a daring rescue of the
little girl sea horse who is held prisoner far away in a deep cave
by an evil crab.
    [1. Sea Horse – Fiction.   2. Marine animals – Fiction]
    I. Bellettati, Riccardo, ill.   II. Title.
    PZ7. D185Lh 1983 [E] 82-20953
ISBN 0-571-12519-0

Printed in Germany

The Little Sea Horse

Story by Mischa Damjan

Pictures by Riccardo Bellettati

ff
faber and faber
Nord-Süd

Simon the little sea horse lived in the southern seas. Like all sea horses he could change his colour; when he was excited he turned red and when he was swimming through forests of green seaweed he turned green. But one thing made him different from all the other sea horses and that was his hobby: he was mad about playing bowls.

Today Simon didn't feel like bowling. Instead he had gone to the coral reef to visit his mother, a famous harpist, who worked in the harp-makers' workshop, tuning the finished harps.

Simon loved the fine silvery notes of the harps. He could hear them from a long way off and they guided him to the workshop door. He was in a good mood as he swam through the seaweed groves.

"How nice of you to come and see me," said his mother. "Have a look round while you're here."

But Simon wasn't listening any more. He was already watching all the sea creatures hard at work. A sawfish was sawing bones and a hammer-headed shark was hammering harps together with whalebone nails. Nimble little fish were spinning fine strands of sea grass to make strings for the harps. Beams of light from a jellyfish lit the whole workshop.

Simon liked Stanley the sawfish best. Stanley was big and strong and Simon would have liked to be his friend, but he was too shy to speak to him.

Simon was so busy watching the harp-makers that he lost track of time. Soon his tummy was rumbling and he began to long for some juicy seaweed.

After his meal Simon curled his tail round a frond of seaweed and fell asleep. He dreamed of a hideous giant fish stunning all the other fish with electric shocks and gobbling them up. Suddenly he turned to chase Simon...

But then Simon woke and found that he had fallen off the seaweed. What a horrible dream! He couldn't sleep any more after that. All around him was darkness. So he swam upwards towards the light.

Simon enjoyed being in the brighter light and he kept on swimming upwards. Suddenly, to his surprise, there was no more water above him. He quickly dived down again, but then curiosity overcame him and he popped his head out of the water once more.

High above him silver lights glimmered and shimmered. They reminded him of starfish. Then one of the lights fell from the sky and plunged into the sea. Simon was horrified. "Are they all going to fall down now?" he wondered. "And is that where starfish come from?"

Simon started to hunt for the light that had fallen. Soon he met a starfish lying on the sandy sea bed.

"Excuse me," said Simon, "have you just fallen from up there?"

At first the starfish didn't understand the question. Then he laughed. "No, silly, I've always been a starfish," he said. "What you saw was a shooting star. Sometimes they do fall into the sea. No one knows where they go – not even the great whale!"

Simon thanked the starfish politely, even though he was disappointed with his reply. On the way home he thought, "I'm sure Stanley could find a shooting star. He's so big and strong; he can do anything."

Next morning there was great excitement on the sea bed. When Simon woke shoals of colourful fish were swimming past him, making the seaweed sway to and fro. A group of mussels had opened their shells wide to ask some passing crabs, "Where is everyone going?" But the crabs didn't answer. They were in too much of a hurry. Even the sea snails and the slow and steady sea cucumbers were hurrying by. Only the angel fish and the box fish stopped to say to Simon, "Come with us. Donald the dolphin has come back!"

Donald the dolphin spent most of his time travelling. But once a year he came to the southern seas to rest from his adventures. Although he was still tired and sleepy Donald said hello to all the sea creatures crowding round his sandy bed.

"Please, Donald, tell us a story," begged his visitors. The dolphin yawned.

"All right," he said. "Far to the north, near the yellow cliffs, a nasty, ugly giant crab is holding a young sea horse called Sally prisoner. Sally's friends have tried to rescue her but they have all failed. The giant crab is too watchful and cunning for them." There Donald stopped.

"Is that all?" squeaked a young sea urchin. "What a silly story, and a gloomy one."

"Tell us one with a happy end," said a sea cucumber.

"I'll tell whatever story I want," mumbled Donald, crossly. "Besides, that story was for Simon, not for cheeky sea urchins." But Simon wasn't listening any longer. The story had made him so sad.

"That's all for today," murmured Donald and went back to sleep.

From that day on Simon felt miserable. He'd lost his appetite and even bowling was no fun any more. All he could think of was poor Sally. Finally he made up his mind: "I'm going to rescue her!"

He went to tell his mother. At first she was horrified, but soon she agreed that it was the right thing to do. She even persuaded Donald and Stanley to help him. Donald and Stanley promised to look after Simon and so the three of them set off.

They swam across undersea meadows, through valleys and over coral reefs. Suddenly they came out of a narrow cleft and saw a beautiful meadow spread out in front of them. It was the meadow where the mysterious sea anemones grew. Simon slid down from Stanley's nose and swam towards one of the deadly sea anemones. He seemed to feel it pulling him closer.

"Get back, Simon. It will eat you!" shouted Stanley and whisked his little friend away before the anemone could grab him.

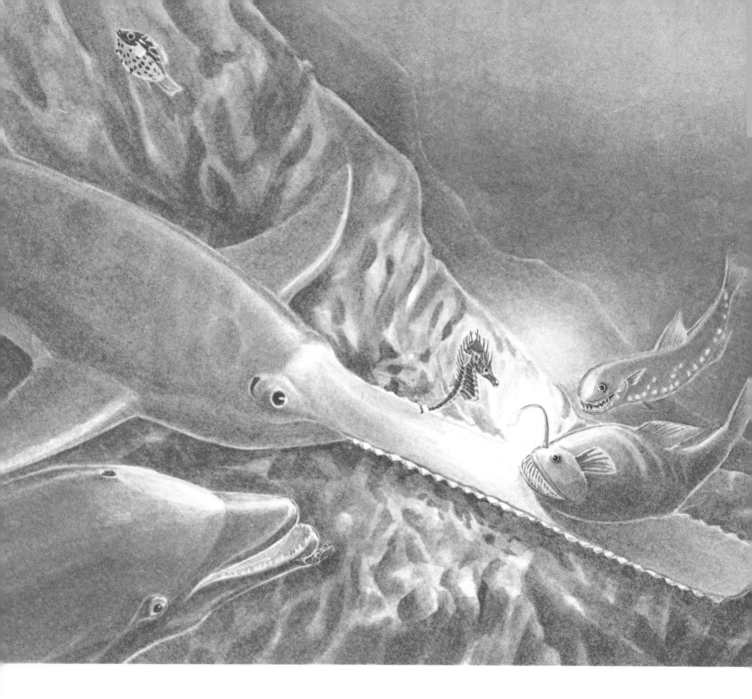

"That was a close one," muttered Donald as they swam quickly onwards.

They travelled on in silence. After a while Donald said, "We're going to need more help." And he told them some more about the giant crab and the deep, dark hollow where she lived.

"The luminous fish could guide us through the darkness," suggested Stanley.

"Good idea. The puffer fish will go and find them for us," said Donald.

They soon met the friendly puffer fish, who showed them where to find the luminous fish. An angler fish and a lantern fish agreed to light their way for them. All five of them swam quickly to the hollow where the giant crab lived. They paused for a moment to make a plan and then the big adventure began.

First the lantern fish began to dance up and down in front of the entrance to the crab's cave. After a few moments they could hear a clattering and a rattling and a scratching as the crab moved about on her spindly legs. Then a horribly shrill voice called out, "What do you want, you wretched fish? Leave me in peace or I'll come out and cut you up!"

But the lantern fish kept on dancing. The crab was very annoyed. She swayed backwards and forwards and snapped her claws menacingly. Then Donald and Stanley darted towards the crab and started to whip the water with their powerful tails.

Simon felt his heart beating wildly. But soon Donald and Stanley had whipped up such a storm that the crab lost her balance and fell onto her back on the sand. Simon took courage. He swam into the dark cave and called, "Quickly, Sally, come with me!" A dainty little sea horse came towards him. She was trembling with fright, but Simon held her tail and led her out of the cave.

Donald and Stanley picked up the little sea horses and swam back to the peaceful valley where the puffer fish lived.

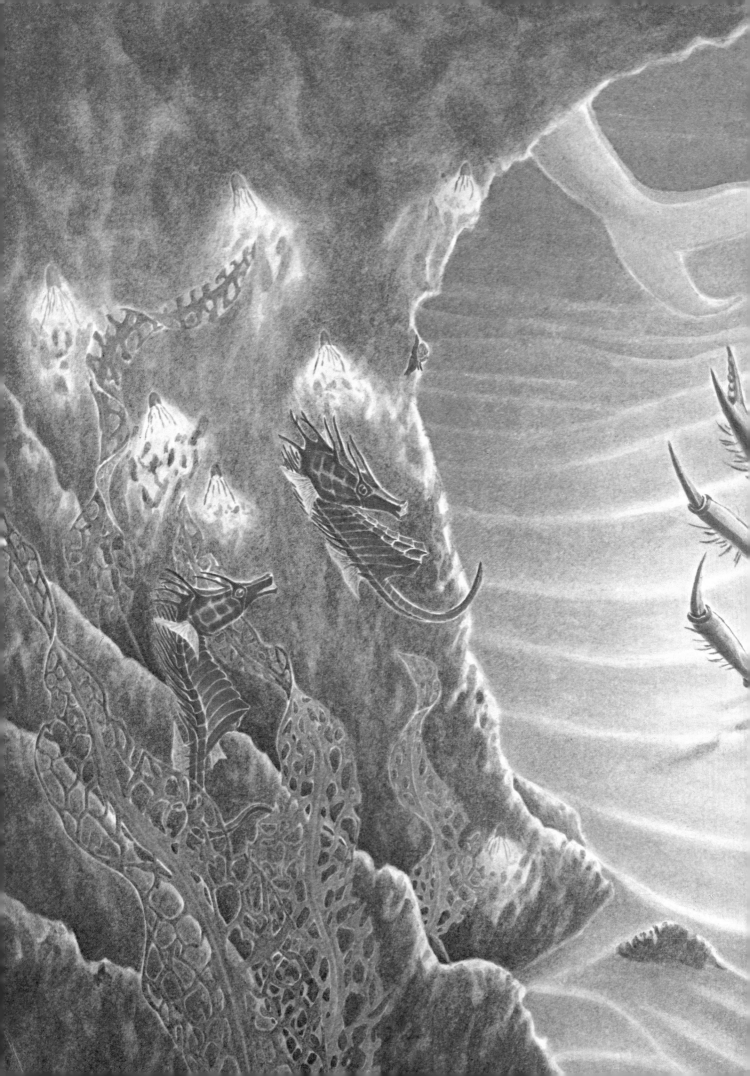

They were tired but happy when they reached the valley of the puffer fish. The sunlit valley was peaceful and the water warm. Stanley and Donald lay on the sand and fell asleep at once. Their efforts in the dark depths had exhausted them. Simon and Sally looked at each other.

"I can't tell you how happy I am to be free again," she whispered, leaning her head against his shoulder. Then they both fell into a deep sleep.

Many hours later they all woke and swam home to find Simon's mother and all their friends waiting for them.